THE PLUM TREE

By Mary Ellen Chase

The Bible and the Common Reader

Dawn in Lyonesse

A Goodly Fellowship

Mary Peters

Silas Crockett

This England

Windswept

Jonathan Fisher:
Maine Parson, 1768–1847

The Plum Tree

THE
PLUM TREE

By

MARY ELLEN CHASE

The Macmillan Company

NEW YORK

1949

This book is dedicated
in gratitude and affection
to
Dr. Justin Hayes
for many years my physician
and my friend

QUID AUTEM EST AMARE, NISI VELLE BONIS
ALIQUEM ADFICI QUAM MAXIMIS, ETIAMSI AD SE EX
IIS NIHIL REDEAT?

*For what, then, is love save to desire all good for
another, even though it bring nothing to oneself?*

Cicero *De finibus* 2.24.

THE PLUM TREE

1

THIS STORY, THE HAPPENINGS AND the thoughts, the pleasure and the sorrow, of these few hours, will run its brief course in a Home for Aged Women, or, as we are given, perhaps euphemistically, to naming such a refuge, in an Old Ladies' Home. Its particular setting, for all stories must be set somewhere, will be a fair-sized American town; and yet it might equally well be placed in London or in Amsterdam, in Rome or in Reykjavik, in Calcutta or in Jerusalem. For the old are everywhere about us and even within us, since, with our first cries, we receive into ourselves the power and the pain, the fancies and the possible wisdom of advanced age. Nor does the actual time of these events matter in the least, for time, in its literal sense, is but a helpful, yet meaningless, division of our sojourns here. Perhaps, indeed, a similar tragedy, or comedy, took place centuries ago, in quite different surroundings and with the peculiar flavor of its own generation.

The protagonist of this fleeting drama is, without doubt, a plum tree. Trees in the long past have often impelled men to action and to thought, invested them with strength and with vision. In the Old Testament days certain trees were held to be sacred, for those who sat or slept beneath them were often strangely enlightened. The golden bough within an ilex tree brought Aeneas safely through the Land of Shadows; the golden apples of another caused a god to forsake the pillars of the sky; and in the leaves of yet another Tree, which, we are told, grows on either side of a boundless River, there is still said to be healing for the nations.

2

On a clear, almost translucent spring morning Miss Angelina Norton, the matron of a Home for Aged Women, and Miss Emma Davis, its nurse, stood by the front window of the matron's office and looked out upon their lawn. It was nine o'clock, and the day was the 15th of May, as the red figures on Miss Norton's neat desk calendar proved beyond a shadow of a doubt. Not that the date, as a date, mattered a whit either to Miss Norton or to Miss Davis, or, if one took a long view of things, would matter a whit to Mrs. Rust, Miss Tiddle, or Mrs. Christianson, whom it very definitely concerned. In other words, it just happened to be the fifteenth day of May, in the year 1948.

Miss Norton and Miss Davis were staring at a little plum tree which grew quite by itself on the lawn and which at that moment was holding the sunlight in every one of its fully blown frail white flowers. The sun, in fact, so enveloped the tree, which was still wet with dew, that it caused a thousand rainbows to gleam and glimmer among its blossoms. Its foaming, shimmering white petals became a pale, shining blue in the still air; it sparkled as though it were flecked with snow crystals and hung with the tiniest of icicles; it looked like a fragment of the Milky Way set with stars and shot through and through with northern lights.

Its glory and radiance there on the green lawn were, Emma Davis thought, almost too much to be endured. She felt, indeed, inside

3

her stiff white uniform something akin to anger against the little tree. "I can't bear it!" she said to herself. "I really can't!" And precisely at the same moment Angelina Norton said the same thing to herself inside her navy blue with white collar and cuffs, while outside them she said to Emma Davis:

"I swear that tree hasn't grown an inch in ten years!"

Miss Davis made no reply, there clearly being none necessary; and each continued to stand in her own window space, one to the right and one to the left, with a broader window between them, and to stare at the little tree.

3

ANGELINA NORTON AND EMMA DAVIS were both not far from threescore years, and neither had been designed, outwardly at least, to startle or to waylay anyone at all. They were both of average height and more than average thickness. They were both a bit broad in the wrong places, a bit heavy in the thighs, somewhat short-legged from the knees down. Miss Norton had scanty brown hair done in an inexpensive permanent, which no one could have mistaken for a natural wave, and rather large, timid brown eyes behind rimless spectacles. Miss Davis had scanty, unwaved gray hair, which her cap mercifully covered, and rather childlike blue eyes, which really needed spectacles, but which Miss Davis could not bear to mar since she thought them her best feature, as indeed they were. Miss Norton's face was surprisingly unlined; Miss Davis', on the contrary, held deep furrows which made circles from her rather good nose around her chin and back again, and from the far corners of her eyes around her somewhat sagging neck. She was deeply conscious of the furrows, which she filled each night with cold cream, to no noticeable improvement.

If any of us should happen to jostle Miss Norton or Miss Davis in the Grand Central or in R. H. Macy's, on Piccadilly or on the Rue de Rivoli, or even in any lesser place (as, in fact, we have done on countless occasions), we would never give either a passing glance, not to mention a passing thought. For about them there was no outward and visible sign that they had plucked golden apples in the Garden of Hesperides, or found the pot of gold at the end of the rainbow, or discovered the golden

5

branch among the shadows, all of which things they had been doing for half a century by the grace of God—which no one truly understands or ever will, least of all Angelina Norton and Emma Davis. Yet these discoveries that they had made in the Garden of Hesperides, which has numberless locations, or at the end of the rainbow, which may be anywhere, or in the Shadows of Hell, which are nearer than next door, had transformed their Home for Aged Women into something quite unlike too many of its counterparts. Because of these discoveries, there was actually an atmosphere of supreme good cheer on nights when the snow fell outside, and the lamps were lighted behind the drawn curtains, and old Mrs. Brown shuffled slowly from her room to show the latest picture of her great-grandson to old Mrs. Jones in bed with sciatica. Because of them, there were early daffodils in the dining room, and laughter at meals, and less irritation at old Mrs. O'Neill, who constantly spilled her soup down her front, belched too often and too noisily, and said *Glory be to God* whenever she did it. Because of them, there was less dread in certain early hours of the dawn in the infirmary at the end of the long corridor when for some old woman the lights grew oddly dim and voices

6

faded quietly away. And lastly, because of them, that pot of gold, that golden bough, and those shining apples hidden away beneath Miss Norton's navy blue and Miss Davis' white, the addled brains of Mrs. Rust, Miss Tiddle, and Mrs. Christianson became at least slightly less addled than of late they had come to be every afternoon at four o'clock.

In other words, Angelina Norton and Emma Davis were wise women, after the saying of that ancient poet and prophet, who wrote that all who seek after Wisdom must forever hunger and forever thirst. Those two were always hungering and thirsting after Something, of which at the moment the little tree on the lawn was a symbol; but just what that Something was they couldn't have told us if they had had all the time in the world, which they hadn't, especially on this fifteenth day of May in the year 1948. They were, as a matter of fact, far wiser than Ecclesiastes, the Preacher, himself an authority on old age and reputedly one of the wisest of men; for his wisdom was based on theory and observation, whereas theirs was grounded on practice and experience. And although their few and unimportant words will never be preserved for centuries, like his own, I will venture to say that they knew far more than he knew about the darkened windows of old eyes, covered with the gray film of cataracts, the trembling of old hands, unable to knit any longer, and the light, fitful sleep of the old in long winter nights when distorted memories weary the mind or cause panic by disappearing altogether.

Yet wise as they were, they both wished they were wiser as they stood at nine o'clock in the morning looking out at the little plum tree and considering the case of Mrs. Melvina Rust, Miss Annie Tiddle, and Mrs. Sigrid Christianson, which in point of fact called for no considering since it had already been settled for good and all exactly thirteen hours before.

4

JUST THEN THE PLUM TREE, CARELESS OF Emma Davis' anger, performed one of those sudden and mysterious acts which blossoming trees and, indeed, countless other things, beautiful or ugly, wholesome or distasteful, are forever accomplishing both to the bewilderment and to the understanding of life. It snatched forty years from the consciousness of Emma

Davis, whisked them quite out of sight, and swept the more distant past into her confused and problematical present. Or perhaps it is more true to say that in one revealing instant it swept away the forty years into far corners of Emma Davis' mind in order to make room for the farther past which had been there all the time, only obscured and often pushed aside. For although, like most of us, Miss Davis did not know it, her beginnings really lived and moved each hour in her present as do the beginnings of us all, though unrecognized and often unseen. In other words, she had no past, but only today and tomorrow, which had been made, and are steadily being made, by the gifts and the laughter, the burdens and the tears, of what we call the past. And in the same instant, by some magical transformation of itself, the plum tree became a girl in a stiff white uniform like Emma Davis' own.

"Hawley," said Emma Davis to herself. "That wretched tree is Hawley to the life."

She seemed still to be standing on a spring morning in her window space, only a few feet from Angelina Norton in hers, and, like Angelina, she was fussing with the cord of the window shade, twisting it, describing its crocheted circlet with her forefinger, swinging it

to and fro; but actually she was sitting at mid-
night in October of the year 1908, on a mass of
rock, behind a great hospital, gleaming with
lights above a great city. A wide, black river
flowed below the rocky heights upon which the
hospital stood. She could see the vague, dim
shapes of boats anchored upon it, outlined by
their riding lights—barges and dredgers,
freighters, tugboats, a steamship or two. She
could see the hospital lights reflected in the
moving water, wavering, shattered into yellow
squares, oblongs, globes, shaking unsteadily
like her own heart inside her blue gingham
uniform. It was her eighteenth birthday, and
she was crying.

A girl named Hawley sat beside her, Jane
Hawley, yet no one called her anything but
Hawley. She wore a white uniform and a cap
with a black ribbon, and she was smoking a
cigarette, concealing its glow as best she could
beneath her heavy nurse's cape. Girls did not
openly smoke cigarettes in the year 1908, and
Emma Davis felt for Hawley a chill of dread
added to her own terrors. Hawley smoked on,
lighting one from another, grinding out the
butts on the rock, and dropping them into the
deep inside pocket of her cape. When she had
exhausted the contents of the ragged pack, she

10

twisted the paper in her hand and dropped it, too, inside her pocket. Then she wrapped a fold of her cape over Emma Davis' shoulders, for the night air was brisk and cold, and Emma was shaking.

"Now, kid," Hawley said, the words echoing still in Emma Davis' ears, "either you take it or you don't. That's for you to say. The big game's up on Monday, and you've made the grade. If you make up your mind you can't take it, you can peddle ribbons somewhere or learn to pound a typewriter. Anyhow, you'll know you've lived in Hell for six months and come out alive. That's something. You've got the best hands and the best head on the wards, you and that scared Norton child. Old Sackett said that to me this morning—she's Satan loose at times, but, believe me, she knows her stuff —'Davis and Norton,' she said to me, 'they've got what it takes, Hawley. The rest we're capping are run of the mill, all right, competent enough—but!' "

Emma Davis at Hawley's words held up her sopping handkerchief to dry in the wind sweeping from the river. She was trying to hear Old Sackett saying those words to Hawley about her and Angelina. She could not.

Miss Davis, haven't you learned yet how to square that sheet properly?

Get on to your job, Miss Davis! I'll inform you when the patients need cheering up.

Step lively now, Miss Davis! A bath takes ten minutes and no more.

That dressing on 19 is a rotten job, Miss Davis. Do it over, and don't take all day.

You turned white in the surgery this morning, Miss Davis, over just that small matter. What'll you do, I ask you, when you see a real one?

Hawley was speaking again.

"It's been a vile birthday for you, all right. I'm sorry you had to see that boy passing out. It's not so bad when they're old."

Emma Davis saw again the long, thin body on the bed, still warm as she and Hawley straightened it out. She saw the lines of the boy's face lose their thought, their knowledge, their bitter pain, grow oblivious, indifferent, calm. He was only eighteen, that boy, and by an odd irony of circumstance he had died on his birthday while on hers she had lived. "It's my birthday," he had said that morning, whispering the words in his swollen throat, picking at the bedspread with his hot fingers. Why

12

must the fingers of the dying always stray about the coverings, pick and fret at their patterns, twist a loose thread here and there? She had helped Hawley wash him, wipe away the sweat, lift his arms, dry them, place them at his side. The blood had pounded in her ears as she had watched Hawley stop the openings of his body, so short a time ago warm with life, passing to her the bits of white cotton with hands which were at that moment colder even than his own.

Then the clean white sheet, the orderlies, the stretcher, the long journey through the corridors to the elevator, the steady, rhythmic tap of feet on hard, clean floors, the purr of rubber wheel tires, the jar of the stretcher as they pushed it into the elevator, the silent, embarrassed crowding together there as they went down and down to the dim, cold room where the dead briefly waited, white forms in bunks around the wall. When she and Hawley had turned away to go back to light and warmth and life, Emma Davis, seized by an uncontrollable impulse, had suddenly reached out her hand and touched one of the straight, silent forms beneath its sheet, in the next bunk to the one in which the orderlies had placed the boy.

13

It was as though she had touched a plank, the trunk of a tree, a stone.

"Don't do that!" Hawley had whispered. "Why, for God's sake, must we all do that?"

"Will I ever forget it all?" Emma Davis now said to Hawley, with the black night around them, the careless stars over their heads, the river far below.

Hawley took a moment to reply, holding the fold of her cape more closely around Emma, against the wind.

"No," she said. "At least, I hope you won't forget. That's what they always say in hospitals. 'You'll forget, you'll shake down, you'll get used to it.' The trouble with most people is that they forget too much, get used to things too quickly. If you forget too much, you'll die a worse death than that boy died, and a longer one. Only remembering won't hurt so much by and by. That's the best I can say to a kid like you."

5

EMMA DAVIS HAD NOT FORGOTTEN—anything. She had not forgotten the terror or the despair or the sadness, nor yet the gaiety, the courage, and the faith of forty years spent with illness, old age, and death. Only in some odd way, through those many years, she had been able, though quite unconsciously, to transcend experience itself into the meaning of it, to capture and to hold the essence, the quality, and the spirit of experience, which, in comparison with the mere recollection of events and circumstances, is the rare miracle of memory, the possible daily changing of water into wine, and within which is healing rather than pain.

On nights when nine o'clock had come, and Miss Annie Tiddle had broken up a game of hearts by falling asleep over it, and everyone still up had had a drowsy cup of cocoa, when back rubs had been given in the infirmary and old Mrs. Cobb's arthritic knee had been coddled by a down pillow, Emma Davis got out of her white oxfords with indulgent groans of pain and of relief, put her aching feet upon a high, soft hassock, and settled down in her room off the infirmary for an hour with the *National Geographic*. The *National Geographic* had been for many years Emma Davis' *vade mecum*. She quite frankly adored reading of places which she would never see, planning journeys for her and Angelina which they

15

would never take. Spain. For some singular and undiscovered reason Emma had mapped out any number of voyages to Spain. There might come a time when she and Angelina would have saved some money, when they might find just the two right women to look after the Home. Then they would shed their navy blue and white, cross the sea, and wander at will through the courts of the Alhambra, accompanied by a guide named, perhaps, Fernando. The beauty of the Alhambra, according to the *National Geographic*, had "defied the description of unnumbered writers"; it was, indeed, "the architectural glory of ancient Granada." They would gaze upon "the rare natural beauty of its situation," "the peaks of the Sierra Nevada in the distance"; they would roam through the "exquisitely graceful" Court of the Lions "with its magnificent alabaster basin supported by twelve lions in white marble." The tiles of this ancient court, once "the winter palace of the Moorish kings," were of blue and yellow, the colonnades of white, and when the brilliant Mediterranean sun flooded all, "the glare dazzled the eyes and confounded the imagination."

The trouble with the *National Geographic*, at least in Emma Davis' hands, was that it

16

never let her stay half long enough where it had taken her. No sooner had she read of the white, blue, and gold in the Court of the Lions, than she was back in the surgery at the hospital, irretrievably, unwillingly there, in *its* glare of white and yellow light. She was in the gallery above, looking down on the white-clad figures below, smelling the pale blue smell of ether, staring at the still body on the table, hearing its heavy, senseless breathing. Her right hand clutched a flask of ammonia in her pocket. If she weathered the first slash of that incredibly small knife, she would take the rest quite easily. It was always the first slash that mattered, that caused the cold, sickening tremor in one's stomach. . . . Or she was down below in the theater, working in that relentless, brilliant glare, in that white silence, watching intently to miss no quick necessity, handing gauze, scissors, forceps in rhythmic succession, so many forceps to clamp the severed blood vessels that they lay on the bared expanse of red flesh in a mass of shining metal like some barbaric decoration.

"Take it easy there," the surgeon said to the anesthetist, who sat on a high stool at the head of the table, as he cut and clamped. His words

17

punctuated the heavy silence like so many stones thrown into a still pool.

Or perhaps, still in Spain, after she and Angelina had lain for hours in the sun and sand of the Bay of Biscay, where, at least earlier in the century, they might have caught a glimpse of the royal Infantas and Infantes (the words fascinated Emma), she would read of religious processions in the Pyrenees, on feast days when all the peasants followed the sacred Host held high in a glittering monstrance in the village priest's hands. She and Angelina, sitting on donkeys, which, according to the *National Geographic*, was the delightful mode of Pyrenean travel, watched the procession from the side of some mountain road, seeing the children scattering flowers, the choirboys singing in white surplices, the women in their bright peasant costumes dangling their rosaries, their lips moving in prayer.

Again, Emma was unceremoniously whisked off her donkey, which she always pictured as more recalcitrant than Angelina's, and set down on her feet by old Mrs. O'Flaherty's bed in the same familiar hospital. Another priest was standing there, older even than Mrs. O'Flaherty. With his right hand he was making the sign of the cross on Mrs. O'Flaherty's wet forehead, while with his left he was covering her hands, which held her rosary.

"We only know that God is merciful, my child," he was saying, "but that is enough."

Just what was *Enough?* Emma would find herself now and again thinking through the years. For it was that baffling word that remained with her, teasing her in her head. Was it possible ever to know Enough of anything? Even of the mercy of God? And just what *was* the mercy of God? Was it, indeed, an ironic nothing, as it often seemed, or, by some strange and ecstatic transformation of one's thoughts, one's mind, was it suddenly Everything?

Or there was Stratford-on-Avon and Shakespeare. The *National Geographic* did not deal much with Stratford-on-Avon, thinking, perhaps, that most readers knew of it and preferring instead to enlighten them concerning the Arctic Circle, the South Seas, the Himalayas, and brilliant flying fish. But Stratford, with Anne Hathaway's cottage and the church by the river where Shakespeare was buried, was firmly placed in Emma's mind, and, after Spain, she and Angelina must surely go there.

Emma Davis owed a great debt to Shakespeare, which, she felt uncomfortably now and again, she had never discharged. Perhaps the

trip to Stratford might cancel it far more pain-
lessly than other more rigorous methods which
thus far had failed. She had had many a bout
with Shakespeare, in all of which she had
ingloriously gone down before him. In simple
words, she could not read his plays, partly because she hadn't time, partly because she fell
asleep over them. This deficiency in her, which
she honestly recognized as a grave and serious
deficiency, was constantly, it seemed, being
brought home to her. If she accompanied Miss
Sophonisba Clark to her literary club, as she
often did, for Sophonisba was growing uncer-
tain on her feet, ten to one the program was on
Shakespeare: *Flowers in Shakespeare*, daffodils,
pansies, oxlips, nodding violets; *Shakespeare's
Knowledge of Women*, Portia, Rosalind, Lady
Macbeth; *Did Shakespeare Write His Own
Plays?* Why ever shouldn't he have written
them? thought Emma, coming suddenly to
herself beside Sophonisba, for she had lost the
trail of this controversial paper in her nagging
anxiety over whether she and Angelina should,
or should not, admit Mrs. Sigrid Christianson
to their Home for Aged Women. And at the
close of these hours with Shakespeare, the pres-
ident of the club invariably said: "Ladies, we

all know far too little of the Immortal Bard. Let us read him more."

Then Emma would once again draw a fat volume in very fine print from the town library, *The Complete Shakespeare*, and take it home with her, opening it night after night and getting hopelessly lost in street scenes in Verona or in Rome where people talked stupidly of *coals*, and *colliers*, *choler* and *collars*, *all* and *awls*, or in lines like:

> *As whence the sun 'gins his reflection*
> *Shipwrecking storms and direful thunders*
> *   break,*
> *So from that spring whence comfort seemed*
> *   to come*
> *Discomfort swells.*

Until Angelina would say a month later:

"We owe a sixty-nine-cent fine on that Shakespeare. That's an extra we really can't afford."

Still, there was the debt. For there were a few brief lines of Shakespeare which Emma Davis knew and could never forget. They always lay in her mind where she could look at their words and say them over and over, realizing sadly (and a bit proudly, perhaps) as she did so that she understood their meaning and their echoes

21

quite as well as had Shakespeare himself understood them. She had learned them years back, in that same omnipresent hospital where she and Angelina had tarried for twelve years until, against all the advice of all the people they knew, they had decided to return to their native town and to take over the tottering Home for Aged Women.

She had learned them from a patient of hers, who, after a long illness, was dying gaily. When all this happened, Emma was only twenty-five, still at an age when a gay death to her meant a strange collision of worlds and was far harder to cope with than death in its more usual aspects. Her patient was a young woman, Mary Knowles her name was, a teacher in a high school. She kept some small red volumes of Shakespeare on her bedside table, and she was forever reading them. Once, when Emma Davis remonstrated with her, suggested the newspaper or a novel instead, she looked up from her pillows and laughed, a laugh which had the peculiar effect of raising a high and insurmountable wall between her and Emma.

"Run along," she said. "I don't need a thing. It's just possible, you see, that Shakespeare won't be in that undiscovered country from whose bourn no traveller returns."

The few lines which remained in Emma Davis' mind she had heard Mary Knowles reciting to herself one night when she had tiptoed to her door to make sure she was asleep. It was a night of quiet spring rain, falling on new, half-opened leaves, bringing dandelions to quick life.

> *We are such stuff*
> *As dreams are made on, and our little life*
> *Is rounded with a sleep.*

Emma had never been able to find the lines, though she had on a dozen occasions hunted for them in *The Complete Shakespeare*; but the day was coming when she would find them. She and Angelina would retire before many years from their Home for Aged Women, turn it over to just the right persons, and live in an apartment of their own. There would be time then to realize many of their dreams, even if these did not include journeys to Spain and to Stratford-on-Avon; and in all that time, those numberless bright hours lying carelessly about, she could, and she would, master *The Complete Shakespeare*.

WHEN THE PLUM TREE CEASED TO BE
Hawley and became itself again, when all the
meanings of that black night above the river
and of the years which followed had redefined
themselves in quick flashes through Emma
Davis' mind, she looked at Angelina still twisting her cord in her window space. A great
tenderness for Angelina swept over Emma at
that moment. She was clearly tired, done in,
washed out. She needed nothing so much as a
day in bed, with hot cups of tea at frequent
intervals, and a solacing magazine with quiet
pictures, *House Beautiful*, *Better Homes and
Gardens*. Her brown eyes behind her spectacles
looked scared, as they had years ago when Old
Sackett had been more on the loose than usual.
Everyone but Emma called Angelina *Angie*,
and, it must be admitted, the diminutive suited
her far more aptly than did her full name. But
Emma stuck to *Angelina*, partly because it
amused her by its very incongruity, largely
because she felt that its frequent utterance
served, in some odd way, as a prop to Angelina.

Emma Davis had been known as *Davy* from
her youth up. She hated the name of *Emma*.
Once you were neatly inside *Emma*, she felt,

there was no getting out. Plop you went in, and plop you stayed. Within the tight blank walls of *Emma* there were no doors opening on enticing vistas such as other names provided, *Eleanor*, for example, *Margaret*, *Dorothy*. And since Emma Davis had never so much as heard of Emma Bovary or Emma Woodhouse, who, in spite of their baptisms, burst their bonds and rose to tragic and to comic stature, her feeling against her name, in her own mind at least, deserves our understanding.

"I'm glad it was your day off yesterday, Davy," Angelina said at last, although she still looked at the plum tree and not at Emma Davis. "I'm soft enough, but you're softer. With you around I don't think I'd have had the guts. But by the time Rusty had called a taxi, and I found Christy in the kitchen actually pulling out drawers to find a bread knife, I knew we were licked. Tiddle was the last straw. She telephoned the undertaker at three o'clock."

"Well, I'm damned!" Emma Davis said. She enjoyed mild profanity from time to time, just as she enjoyed the countless lies she found it necessary to fabricate. "I'm damned!" she repeated. "She never did!"

"She did. Right in the front hall with everybody listening. 'I'm dying at four,' she said. 'Come at four-thirty and get my remains. The clothes you're to put on me are in a box with *Sanitary Laundry* on the cover. And see that you treat me with respect, for I was somebody once, even if I'm nobody now.' She'd got that far before I could get upstairs and take her to her room. And then everybody broke loose. Mrs. Wilcox was having callers, and she was embarrassed to death; the two Wood sisters sent for me and said they hadn't reckoned on coming to an insane asylum; and Emily Goddard said she'd apparently entered under a misunderstanding and meant to change her will at once, even if she couldn't persuade her nephews to take her out, which she devoutly hoped she could.

"Then just before supper the Seventies called on me in a body, all eight of them, and pushing along old Mrs. Whipple in her wheel chair. They were quite calm and dignified and, of course, terribly important. They let Whipple do the talking. It took her ages in her precise way. 'Miss Norton,' she said, 'this deputation of ladies regrets exceedingly that it must wait upon you concerning a matter so painful to us all and so damaging to the name of the Home for Aging Women.' I think that was it. I know

26

she said *aging* as she always does. She was very elegant, of course, as she always is, and thoroughly enjoying herself. She ended by saying that the Seventies had more reason to complain than the Eighties, being, as she put it, 'less subject to the ravages of time.' "

"I'm sorry I missed it," Emma Davis said. "Whipple can put on a show, wheel chair and all."

"Well, it was one show too many," Angelina Norton said. "I guess supper was glum enough, finnan haddie, too. I didn't go; I couldn't face it. I had trays sent to Rusty, Christy, and Tiddle. I will say they were quiet by that time. Then I sent for the doctors, Gray, of course, and Bright and Williams from the State Hospital. I got hold of Susan Pierce, too, and told her that if she'd ever loved us in all these years, to get along down here. 'I can't take three men singlehanded,' I said to her, and down she came. If it hadn't been for her and the things she said to them about what we've been trying to do in this place for thirty years, I couldn't have stood it. Well, by eight o'clock everything was settled. There being no relatives, it didn't take long."

"Committed, I suppose," Emma Davis said. "And for keeps, of course."

27

Angelina Norton still twisted the cord of the window shade, still stared at the little tree.

"They don't say that. They always say, *observation;* but it doesn't mean a thing. Anyhow, let's hope the 'keeps' aren't too long. They're all over eighty."

"But tough," Emma Davis said. "I know their insides like an open book. Tiddle's the toughest. Her heart's not a day over fifty-five. And Christy's a Swede, don't forget. They're made of iron, Swedes are. The only hope is Rusty. She hasn't too much to go on, I'm glad to say."

7

WHILE ANGELINA NORTON AND EMMA Davis had been talking, each in her own window space, with the larger window between them, two little girls had been skipping rope on the sidewalk just beyond the stretch of green lawn before the Home for Aged Women. They were just two nameless little girls, six and seven years old perhaps, with white socks and scuffed brown shoes, very short blue chambray frocks, pigtails tied over each ear with blue bows, and quite likely, if they had been close enough to be clearly seen, spaces in their mouths where they had lost their first teeth. Now, just as Angelina Norton and Emma Davis had stopped talking to ponder for a bit over those mysterious and troubling gifts which Life and Time had bestowed so generously upon Mrs. Rust, Miss Tiddle, and Mrs. Christianson, they stopped swinging their ropes and advanced hand in hand across the lawn toward the little plum tree. When they got quite close to it, they stood, still hand in hand, and gazed at it as though they were too surprised to move or to speak. Their faces were uplifted to it there in the sunlight, and Emma Davis saw, or feared she saw, a new world, or perhaps the understanding of an old one, opening before their eyes. She feared that water was again being changed into wine, that power and glory and pain were getting inside the blue chambray frocks, and she thought she couldn't bear it.

"Don't, my darlings!" her heart cried out to them. "Run away. Don't look too long! It's too soon. Run away, I say!"

And as though the little girls had heard the warning of Emma Davis' heart, they did run away across the wet lawn and on to the sidewalk again.

8

I DON'T NEED TO TELL YOU," ANGELINA
said, once the little girls had safely gained the
sidewalk to her immense relief also, "that those
psychiatrists or neurologists or whatever else
they call themselves up there in the State Hospital haven't a high opinion of you and me,
Davy, in spite of all Susan Pierce managed to
tell them. They think we've been sacrificing
the safety of the many for the comfort of the
few. In other words, they don't think we've
been very ethical."

"I don't give a damn what they think,"
Emma Davis said. "Ethics just don't work in a
home for old ladies, or at least what most
people call ethics. We've been minding our
own business and making out very well. After
all, it wasn't till yesterday that Christy tried
to get anything to work with. She's just talked
before, and not to many at that. Harmless
enough, she's been, and everybody's felt just
sorry. And I've always been able to manage
Rusty. She just packs and unpacks, and it keeps
her busy. As for Tiddle—well, I must say I
think Tiddle's calling the undertaker was a
scream. Laugh when you can in this place, I

say. There are plenty of tears. . . . Well, when's the Exodus?"

Angelina Norton seized the window sash with her square, capable hands before she answered Emma Davis. She obviously felt the need of support.

"It's at four today," she said. "When I told the doctors about all the things that have been happening around here at four o'clock for the last two weeks, they apparently thought that was the hour. I suppose it's reasonable enough. From what they said, or didn't say, I gathered they wanted to see the three of them while the notions are still on."

Emma Davis turned from the window and the view of the little plum tree as rigidly and abruptly as though she were a mechanical toy. Now she stood at right angles to both and stared at Angelina, who still held on to the sash.

"You and I aren't likely to forget the hour of four, Angelina, for the rest of our mortal lives," she said. "I always used to think it was the dullest hour of the twenty-four, but never again! And since what will be, will be, I'll get busy. I suppose, knowing you, the day's a Special?"

"It is," Angelina said. "Last night, after the

doctors had gone, and I knew what was what, I got the Seventies together and told them the whole mess. I knew they'd stand by, once they understood. They all cried a little, and said we could bank on them. They're all nice old things, really, and the two other Eighties out of bed won't matter. They'll just follow along. There's going to be roast chicken for dinner. We can't afford it, but I don't care. And I've ordered ice cream in molds, roses in strawberry for everyone except O'Neill and McCarty, who get shamrocks in pistachio. I'm going to place the three tables in one big square, and, for God's sake, Davy, don't let me down. You've got to make things go. I'm like it says in the Prayer Book—there's no health left in me."

There was just the slightest suspicion of a tremor in Angelina Norton's lips as she completed this rather long explanation; but it had no time to develop into a full-fledged tremble. For just at that moment, while she fingered the window sash, and Emma Davis stood at right angles to her, and the plum tree continued to grow in grace if not in height, a sound was heard in the room above them as though someone with great determination were dragging a heavy object across the floor. Emma Davis did not tarry to assure Angelina that she wouldn't let her down, but, since she hadn't once done so in thirty years, Angelina really required no confirmation. Instead, she started for the doorway with a crisp sound of cleanliness and starch, bound straight, as Angelina Norton well knew, for the room of Mrs. Melvina Rust.

"Just a moment, Davy," Angelina said, turning quickly from her window space. "There's nothing happening up there that hasn't happened every day for a fortnight. You haven't told me a thing about what you did yesterday."

Emma Davis turned from the open doorway and faced Angelina's accusing eyes. She tried to be nonchalant and easy, and she failed. She stood there, looking at Angelina, readjusting her cap, running her forefinger under a pleat of her uniform which needed loosening from its load of starch.

"First, I had my hair done," she said. "I shouldn't have, but I did. It's getting thin on the left side, so now it's parted on the right and curled. Of course, you haven't noticed. Then I had supper at Ferry's. Oyster stew and very good. It cost sixty-five cents. Then I went to the movies and saw a picture called *A Night to Remember*. It was very silly, and I liked it. You wouldn't have. Is that all?"

"No," said Angelina. "You shopped. Whatever is in that big box under this desk? It's marked *Fragile*."

"That's just right," Emma Davis said. "It is fragile. It's so fragile you could crush it in your hands without half trying. It's a tea set."

"A tea set!" cried Angelina Norton, forgetting for the moment in her consternation all the far weightier happenings of yesterday, all the ominous dread of today, and advancing from her window space quite up to Emma. "What in the world for?"

Emma Davis all at once stopped fussing at her cap, the front pleat of her uniform. Her hands fell at her sides; her body became rigid; her slowly widening blue eyes stared at Angelina, but saw her not; her mouth dropped open. She stood in the matron's office of the Home for Aged Women, in that neat, brisk room where they had conferred together for thirty years; but in reality she was on some Mount Peor like the ancient seer, who, falling into a trance with his eyes wide-open like Emma Davis' eyes, had, like her, a vision of his immediate future straight and clear before him.

"That's just what I wondered yesterday," she said, spacing each of the words as though she were discovering each, one by one, and setting each down carefully in its appointed

34

place. "What in the world for? I asked, just as you're asking now. Well, now I know what for. It's a lovely tea set, white, like that little tree with tiny pale green leaves, and fragile, as it says on the box. And you'd better unpack it right away, for, mark my words, we're going to need it before this day is over. . . . And now," she concluded, descending suddenly from Mount Peor and starting toward the doorway as the sounds above increased in haste and violence, "I have various things to do. You can dock the price from my salary. It cost $8.75, and it's going to be worth every penny of it—and more."

9

NOW MRS. MELVINA RUST, TOWARD whose room Emma Davis was hastening, had once lived in a small white house at No. 14 Vine Street, an inconsequential house enough, with sagging green shutters and frayed gingerbread work over its front door. There was no longer any such house on Vine Street, nor had there been for ten years, it having been sold to the owner of a filling-station, who had paid exactly enough money for it to get Mrs. Rust at seventy-two into the Home for Aged Women. But although Mrs. Rust had known this fact quite clearly in the beginning and for a long time thereafter, of late it had strayed away somewhere. In her mind, instead, the house was still there on Vine Street, still belonged to her, and still had a red geranium in the parlor window which still needed her care. To be sure, up to a few weeks ago Mrs. Rust had been willing to believe in a tenant at 14 Vine Street named Mrs. Hawkins, who, according to Emma Davis, took excellent care of the house, the polyanthus under the dining-room window, and the pippin tree in the back yard. But just lately Mrs. Hawkins had gone so far back into Melvina Rust's mind that there was no bringing her out again. She was hidden there under dark, thick layers of forgetfulness, together with Mr. Rust, who had died long ago, and a nephew called Melvin, who had done so badly by his aunt and uncle and his world at large that he had years back been moved to a place where there were no possessions of others for him to get his hands upon.

That was, in short, Mrs. Rust's story; but the only parts of it which were now real to her were that her house still stood at 14 Vine Street and that she must return to it each afternoon at four o'clock. Every day for a fortnight now she had gotten ready to go, and every day she had been kept from going, sometimes by a threatening thunderstorm, so graphically described by Miss Davis that it would have been madness to venture out, sometimes by a sore throat, which Miss Davis discovered just in the nick of time, sometimes by household mending, or preparing vegetables, or running the dustmop in the corridor, duties which had so piled up on Miss Norton, or the cook, or Miss Davis that they simply could not manage to exist unless Mrs. Rust could postpone her return home in order to help them out. But today, with the sky blue and the air mild and that little plum tree, which Mrs. Rust could see from her window, full of blossoms, was clearly the day; and Mrs. Rust had made up her mind, or what was left of it, that she was going back to 14 Vine Street for good and all, and she was beginning to pack her belongings in her old canvas carryall. She was, therefore, inclined toward rebellion when Emma Davis burst through her door, for she had had some reason in the near past to suspect Miss Davis.

"Rusty!" Emma Davis cried with no preliminaries whatever and no apparent notice of the carryall on the floor. "My dear Rusty, the most extraordinary thing has happened, the most completely extraordinary thing! Two, in fact, but we'll take them one at a time. Sit down in that chair by the window where you can see that little plum tree, for what I'm about to tell you, Melvina Rust, is every bit as exciting as that little tree."

Mrs. Rust moved slowly toward the chair, but she kept a wary eye on the carryall and on Miss Davis.

"You needn't tell me there's going to be a thunder shower today," she said, "for I can see with my own eyes there isn't. I haven't a sore throat, and I'm not doing any mending for you. I'm going home at four o'clock, and that's that!"

Emma Davis settled old Mrs. Rust in the chair and knelt beside her on the floor. She looked big beside Mrs. Rust, who was a little woman with shaking hands and vague blue eyes and scraggly gray hair in curlpapers.

"I wouldn't stop you for worlds, Rusty," she said. "There couldn't be a better day for a journey; but before you pack, you've got to hear my news. I'm bursting with it, and so is Miss Norton. There's going to be a Special dinner today to celebrate it. Rusty, it's about

Melvin. You'd never believe the honors he's brought you!"

"Melvin?" said Mrs. Rust. "Now who might Melvin be?"

"Now, Rusty," Emma Davis said, drawing a long breath. "Don't pretend. You know very well that you remember Melvin. You remember how you brought him up, and how once he set fire to Snooks, the white-haired dog, and how you had to spank him for it, and how he never could get enough of your famous apple dowdy. Don't tell me you don't remember that handsome Melvin Rust, for I *know* you do!"

It was Emma Davis' knowledge that accomplished the miracle. For suddenly, far below the layers of almost complete oblivion which made up most of Mrs. Rust's mind, some faint light flickered, wavered, glowed for an instant, struggled to pierce the darkness, and finally managed a frail streak through it, like a beacon through almost impenetrable fog.

"I guess perhaps I do," Mrs. Rust said. "I guess anyway I remember how he ate too much of that apple dowdy and had to take castor oil. How old is Melvin now? Fifteen, perhaps?"

"Melvin is twenty-six," Emma Davis said firmly, thinking more quickly than she had ever thought in all her life. "You forget how

39

time flies, Rusty. *Tempus fugit*, you know, as you and I learned in school. Yes, Melvin Rust is twenty-six, and he is now Captain Melvin Rust, chief aide and counselor to General Mac-Arthur himself. He is in Tokyo, Japan, Rusty. There's a letter from him in Miss Norton's office that tells us all about it. Miss Norton is so impressed that she's having copies made of it for everyone, and one will be read aloud at dinnertime. He wrote her only because he didn't know whether you were here or at 14 Vine Street, and, though he was modest about himself, it's easy enough to see just how important Melvin is. Why, Rusty, that letter is clearly marked: *General MacArthur's Headquarters, Tokyo, Japan.* Rusty, can you believe it? That nephew of yours who set fire to Snooks and got sick on your apple dowdy?"

Mrs. Rust sat up very straight and began to unwind her curlpapers.

"Well, I never did!" she said. "That Melvin! I must say it's a surprise. Is that war still going on? I thought there were those V-Days long ago when we had ice cream and hung out the flag."

"There's always a war going on some-where," Emma Davis said. She stopped for the fraction of a second to savor this grim truth in her own mind; but she couldn't stop long, for everything depended upon her gathering together Mrs. Rust's scattered wits and holding them for her against their getting loose again. "But you're quite right, Rusty. That war is over, thank God. Only General MacArthur can't leave Tokyo quite yet, and, of course, Melvin has to stay with him, for it's very plain that the general can't move hand or foot without your nephew."

"Well, I never!" said Mrs. Rust again, still hurriedly taking off more curlpapers and letting little wisps of curls loose on her rather bald old head. "I must say I never would have believed it of that Melvin. I never would! It just shows you never can tell what's going to happen in this world."

"You most certainly cannot!" Emma Davis said, savoring the truth of this statement also. "But I, for one, always thought that Melvin had it in him. He'll be a four-star general yet, Rusty—mark my words! All you did for him as a boy is just coming out, as I always knew it would. But I haven't told you all, Rusty, dear. Now stop taking off those curlpapers and listen hard. Captain Melvin Rust, who everyone is going to know about at dinner today, has sent you the most beautiful present, way from Tokyo, Japan. It's a tea set, Rusty, the most

41

wonderful tea set of the frailest, daintiest pure white china with little sprigs of pale green leaves, six cups, six saucers, six plates, a cream pitcher, a sugar bowl, and a teapot. It's just the color of that little plum tree and just as gay. Miss Norton and I have unpacked it, and we're going to have it on display at our dinner party, so that everyone can see it and so that everyone can know how much Captain Rust thinks of his Aunt Melvina."

By this time two bright red spots had appeared on Mrs. Rust's wrinkled cheeks. She was sitting up straight in her chair with curlpapers off and curlpapers on, and there were tears in her blue eyes.

"Well, I really never did!" she said. "And coming on the very day I'm going home for good! I assume," she concluded, with just the merest trace of returning suspicion, "that I'll be allowed to take my own tea set, sent me by my own nephew, to my own home with me?"

Emma Davis laughed aloud and placed her strong, broad hands over Mrs. Rust's small, shaking ones.

"If you aren't allowed to take that tea set when you go this afternoon, my name's not Emma Davis," she said; "but Rusty, I've got a marvelous idea. Don't you think it would be

42

nice, and really the proper thing to do, for you to give a very small, very select, tea party up here, say at three o'clock, in honor of Captain Melvin Rust? Honor deserves honor, if you know what I mean. The party needn't be a long one, and, as there are only six cups and saucers, it would have to be small. I wouldn't pack all my things right now, for you'll want your room nice for the party. I'll promise to help you pack afterward."

Old Mrs. Rust was by this time sitting on the edge of her chair with every curlpaper off.

"I must say I think it's a lovely plan," she said. "I've always maintained there's nothing stays the heart like a nice cup of tea." Just then the faintest shadow crept into her eyes, which did not for a moment escape the quick glance of Emma Davis, still kneeling on the floor by Mrs. Rust's chair. "Who'll we ask to this tea party?" asked old Mrs. Rust with again just a hint of suspicion.

Emma Davis rose then and moved closer to Mrs. Rust's window, which looked out on the green lawn and the little tree. She chose her words carefully.

"Miss Norton, of course," she said. "We couldn't have a real party without her. And me, I hope, Rusty. I'd be brokenhearted if I wasn't asked. Now, let's see. It's your party, of course, but what about Miss Tiddle and Mrs. Christianson? I think they'd be awfully pleased and proud to be invited. I've noticed that they've been a little slighted just lately in some of the get-togethers. Or am I just imagining that?"

A deep and portentous silence followed Emma Davis' question. It seemed to her to last for countless minutes, but she neither broke it nor turned from the window. Mrs. Rust rose from her chair then and very stealthily moved across her room to the door. The door was securely closed, but Mrs. Rust drew a key from the pocket of her black sateen apron, fitted it cautiously in the lock, and as cautiously turned it. Then she quietly tried the door, once, twice, three times. Once she was convinced it was locked, she returned to Emma Davis, who had not moved from the window or seemingly paid the slightest attention to Mrs. Rust. She put her arm around Miss Davis' waist before she began whispering in her ear.

"I have something very serious to tell you," old Mrs. Rust whispered to Emma Davis. "I don't want to tell you because you are young, and you shouldn't hear such things. If I didn't think I ought to tell you, I never, never would.

I'm not one that bears false witness against my neighbors. I never, never did at 14 Vine Street, and I never, never shall once I'm back there. It's something about Annie Tiddle and Sigrid Christianson that no one knows but me. And I wouldn't tell it to you, only it's been revealed to me that I must. But before I tell it," Mrs. Rust whispered on, "you'll have to swear on God's Own Word that it shall be a secret between me and thee."

She crept to a small table beside her bed and brought a worn Bible to Emma Davis.

"Put your right hand on this book," she whispered. "The left is not genuine. Only the right will do. Swear that what I'm going to reveal will never be revealed, that what I'm going to speak will never be spoken. Swear!"

"I swear!" Emma Davis said, placing her right hand on the Bible and at the same time encircling old Mrs. Rust with her left arm, for she was now shaking quite too much to be at all firm on her feet.

Mrs. Rust drew still nearer to Emma Davis' ear.

"Mrs. Christianson and Miss Tiddle must be watched," she whispered. "As it says in this book, *I say unto you, Watch.* And since I'm leaving today and can't watch any longer, you must. They've both got queer notions. I don't like to tell you, but it's true. They've both got queer notions about four o'clock. Mrs. Christianson, poor thing, thinks she's been ordered to kill someone at just four. And poor Annie Tiddle thinks she's had a summons. She said to me—though I can't recall just when, but she did, upon my word—'Melvina,' she said, 'I'm dying at four, if not today, then tomorrow. I know it,' she said. Those were her very words. Now did you ever hear anything so awful and so sad?"

Emma Davis led Mrs. Rust back to the chair and placed her securely in it. Then she knelt again on the floor and put her arms around the old woman.

"Rusty," she said, "you're always so wise and kind. I can always depend on you. That's just what it is, *sad*. And, of course, you'd see it as a lot wouldn't. A lot of people would leave Mrs. Christianson and Miss Tiddle alone, poor things, when you and I understand that what they need is friends. Now, because no one knows this but you and me, because it's a solemn secret between us, the only thing for us to do is to work together. We'll ask Mrs. Christianson and Miss Tiddle to your party. They'll be so happy that there won't be any room in

46

their minds to worry about this silly four o'clock. For once you get your mind full of pleasant things, there's just no room for anything that's sad. You see that, Rusty, don't you?"

Old Mrs. Rust did not answer Emma Davis' question. She began instead to look puzzled and distraught, as though she were mightily concerned about an idea that had just occurred to her.

"About that four o'clock," she whispered. "People sometimes steal notions from others, that is, if they get queer and notional like Mrs. Christianson and Annie Tiddle. Perhaps—I don't like to think they would—but just perhaps—they've stolen four o'clock from me."

Emma Davis rose to her feet and stood, strong and dependable, by old Mrs. Rust's chair.

"Nonsense!" she said, her voice full of strength and assurance. "Stuff and nonsense, Rusty! Your four o'clock is yours, and their four o'clock is theirs, and it's all quite clear and simple. Now, dear, if you'll lend me that key, which I'll be careful to return to you, I'll get going. And as I'm passing right by their doors anyway, I'll pop in and invite Annie Tiddle and Mrs. Christianson to your party at just

three. And because it's going to be a very exciting and lovely day, I want to get you properly
ready for it. You can't even see your new tea
set till you've had a good rest. Get your clothes
off now and into that bed, for you're having
the back rub of your life in just half an hour."
She bent over old Mrs. Rust, who was fumbling
for the door key in her black sateen pocket.
"And I'll not forget," she whispered, "that no
one knows a thing about this but only you and
me."

10

ONCE EMMA DAVIS HAD LEFT OLD MRS.
Rust's room for that of Miss Annie Tiddle, she
was acutely conscious of the need for time, for
just ten minutes, five, to pull herself together,
to get a tighter grasp on things in general as
well as on things in particular, to marshal her
scattered faculties of invention and pretense;
but there clearly wasn't any time. Not only
was the journey from the one room to the other
brief in itself, but there were obligations to be
met along the way. All the doors of all the
rooms were open on this bright spring morn-

48

ing; all the occupants of all the rooms were enjoying, or at least accepting, the sun, the fresh, lively air, the kindly drifting in of the light spring wind. Mrs. Cobb was dusting her bric-a-brac: the pink shell which she had herself picked up on her honeymoon at Palm Beach fifty years ago; the miniature Statue of Liberty from the World's Fair in Chicago in 1893; the trio of monkeys who, with their hands in the appropriate places, daily warned Mrs. Cobb to hear, see, and speak no evil. As she dusted, she sang a bit off-key of that sweet hour of prayer that called her from a world of care. "I'm glad to see you looking so well this lovely morning, Mrs. Cobb. Don't forget to look at the little plum tree! It's never been lovelier." Mrs. Goddard and Miss Cora Wright were very consciously resuming a rather solemn game of double Canfield in Miss Wright's window space. "I'm glad to see you two busy people really relaxing on this nice morning. People just don't relax often enough." Old Mrs. O'Neill was about to do up a medal of the Sacred Heart against her great-granddaughter's approaching first Communion. "It needs a bit of shining up, Theresa, my dear. Tooth paste will do it—yes, just tooth paste. Most people don't know what a godsend tooth paste is in a pinch. I can get my tube for you in just a jiffy. And I've a scrap of pretty paper with some angels blowing trumpets. Just the thing for little Agnes. If you could wait a few minutes, say half an hour at the longest, I'll be back."

Emma Davis, as she traversed her interrupted way toward Miss Tiddle's room, was distinctly aware of an atmosphere of tension on that long corridor. There was suspicion about, lurking in the corners; there was fearful excitement hidden beneath the bibs of morning aprons; there was more than a trace of anxious resentment in old eyes looking into her own. All the more necessity, then, for her darting in and out of rooms, for bright comments on the spring day, for the bestowal of quick interest, a favor here and there.

When she once arrived at Miss Tiddle's room, she found the door closed and a sign upon it. *Engaged*, the sign read, in Annie Tiddle's best Spencerian, *Kindly do not enter here*. Emma Davis knocked quickly, the airiest of knocks with her thumb and two fingers, a knock twice repeated like a pair of three grace notes, blithe, merry, vivacious. Then she turned the knob and pranced into Miss Tiddle's

50

grave and somber presence like some young colt bursting through a pasture fence.

"My dear Annie Tiddle," she cried, "forgive me! As you must know by this time, I'm not one to open doors when there are signs upon them. But time is so precious to me this lovely morning, and I've so much to do that I really couldn't help it. You *will* forgive me, won't you?"

If any power on earth, under it, or above it, could have been allowed to dampen the effervescent (if counterfeited) spirits of Emma Davis at that moment, Annie Tiddle's room and Annie herself would have dampened them, indeed soaked them, bogged them down, never to rise again. Miss Tiddle's room was divested of all her personal possessions: her pictures, photographs, all her many Christmas and Easter cards, all her Valentines which she had heretofore kept conspicuously arranged on her mantelpiece; her flower vases, her sewing basket, her rose jar with petals gathered years ago but still sweet; her playing cards always in evidence on her table, for Annie had dearly loved a game of hearts; her books, *Daily Thoughts for Daily Needs*, Longfellow's *Tales of the Wayside Inn*, all the few other volumes from her small bamboo bookcase; her wonder-

fully wrought sofa pillows, tidies, antimacas-
sars, pincushions. All these were apparently
now housed in pasteboard boxes and cartons
which were piled on the floor at the foot of her
bed, all tied up with stout twine, all labeled
with tags in her careful handwriting. On the
very top of the neat pile was a box marked
Sanitary Laundry. It bore a long envelope in-
scribed, *Open when all is over*. The only objects
in evidence, except for those necessary furnish-
ings which the Home supplied its tenants,
were, as Emma Davis' nervous scrutiny instantly revealed, a silent alarm clock on the
bare mantelpiece with its stopped hands point-
ing to four o'clock, a Bible on the lap of Miss
Tiddle, who sat by her window, and Miss Tiddle herself in a neat black dress.

Emma at once crossed the small room, drew
up a chair opposite to Miss Tiddle, and sat
down. She did not convey the least surprise
over the unaccustomed appearance of the
room, or seem to notice the parcels at the foot
of the bed, or apparently recognize the fact that
she was an unwelcome caller. As a matter of
fact, however, that silent clock on the mantel
was making its inroads upon her, and those inroads she must *not* give in to. A silent clock, she
thought, in just the moment she allowed her-

self before she began to combat within her its still face, is anything more ominous and unreal than a silent clock? The voluntary silencing of its hours ticking away: six o'clock, the awaking to a new day, sun or rain or falling snow; noon, the breaking of bread at countless pleasant tables; four o'clock, the scampering of feet freed from school?

"I must not look at that awful clock!" Emma Davis said to herself, while at that very instant she said brightly to Annie Tiddle, "It's unforgivable, my bursting in like this and interrupting you at your reading, but when I once tell you why I've come—"

Miss Tiddle interrupted Emma Davis politely, for she always was polite, but firmly. As she did so, Emma saw with pain the marks of strain in her brown eyes and the nervous twitching of her eyebrows.

"I'm afraid it doesn't matter to me why you've come," she said. "Nothing today can be allowed to come between me and my reading." She hesitated for the small fraction of a minute. "I'm reading St. Paul on death," she concluded. " 'O Death, where is thy sting? O grave, where is thy victory?' "

"I know," said Emma Davis. "Those are wonderful words, and true, too."

My God, she thought frantically, how true they may turn out to be! If I don't get on top of this situation in another few seconds, those wretched questions will be answered once and for all. The sting will quite clearly be with me till the end of my days, and Annie Tiddle will walk off with the victory!

She looked desperately out of Miss Tiddle's window, and there was the plum tree. She had forgotten it for the moment, allowed it to be driven from her mind by that monstrous clock, that stripped room, Annie Tiddle, and St. Paul. There it was, its shadow, as the sun mounted, creeping more closely around it like a circle of surrounding light, and on that shadow a few white petals had fallen.

"I've come to you, Annie, dear, for help," she said quietly. "Just think of all the help you've given me since I was in that third-grade room of ours at school, how kind you were then to all of us. Don't I remember the hours you took, the patience you always had?"

That was true, she thought, that, at least, was true. Miss Tiddle, as Emma Davis' teacher fifty years ago in this very town, had been patient to the point of complete inertia. Her meek patience had, in fact, saddened a long succession of restless children, a great crowd of ruth-

54

less witnesses who unwillingly encompassed her about as she ran her weary, resigned, and uneventful course. For Annie Tiddle, as she ran that course, could not cast aside every weight that easily beset her. There were quite too many of them, as Emma Davis knew: an ailing and complaining mother, lack of money and of friends, a want of humor, of that trifling nonsense which might now and again have turned even *her* Valley of Baca into an occasional well of water. Unlike Mrs. Melvina Rust, she had not had so much as a red geranium in her parlor window or a polyanthus in her backyard, simply because there had been cruelly left out of her that kind and eager necessity which would have placed them there. Nor had she been granted the gift of a thoroughly bad nephew to feed and worry over and, at last, to break her heart upon.

Indeed, these last ten years in the Home for Aged Women had given Annie Tiddle the only happiness she had known, a late benison of security in a frightened, resentful life. She even had come close to blossoming there like some century plant bursting into long-delayed bloom. She had loved the Sunday evening sings around the piano, with Emma Davis' square hands pounding on the keys, *Sun of my soul,*

Thou Saviour dear, Joy to the world! the Lord is Come.

"Miss Tiddle, you take the second soprano here. No one can do it so well as you! Your voice gets better and better."

She had looked forward to the evening cocoa parties with their pleasant talk.

"I almost forgot to tell you, Miss Tiddle, that Mr. Sims, the grocer, asked for you today. He's never forgotten how you used to tie his muffler for him."

She had added many a cubit to her inconsequential stature when, once they had sat down to hearts, Mrs. Whipple, or Mrs. Goddard, or the rather distant Miss Sophonisba Clark would say with an audible sigh: "Well, we may all as well give up at once if Annie Tiddle's going to play. Luck is always with Annie."

And yet a scant ten years had not been quite enough to dim the memory or to deplete the strength of six times their number. There they still were, those sixty years, like rocks cropping up again in a field which you had believed cleared of them for good and all, like crab grass among the new-sown clover and lawn seed, like loathsome, persistent aphids on a rose just ready to flower.

Emma Davis remembered all these things as

she saw with untold relief a faint light creep into Miss Tiddle's bewildered, yet wary brown eyes. By some fortuitous, yet blessed, chance, she had said the one right thing out of a possible dozen which would have been disastrous beyond repair.

"I think I always did have patience," Annie Tiddle said, closing her Bible, to Emma Davis' unspeakable joy, upon St. Paul's rhetorical questions, his glorious certainties. "At least, I did my best with you all. And I may say it's given me heart-warming rewards in years since then. Those many cards sent to me—you recall them, I'm sure. They're in a box with your name on it—just a little memento which I thought you'd like to keep to remember me by."

Emma Davis recalled with no difficulty the many cards. She had once seen Miss Tiddle in Woolworth's buying cards, Valentines those were, and she had concealed herself hurriedly behind the kitchen ware so that Miss Tiddle's own house of cards might not come tumbling down, never to rise again. She had the next morning gathered the cards together as she sorted the mail, noted their thinly disguised handwriting, studied them later on Miss Tiddle's mantelpiece with exclamations of pleasure and approval. *To dear Miss Tiddle, with everlasting thanks. To my Valentine, Miss Tiddle, with enduring appreciation.*

"I shall keep them always," she said to Miss Tiddle, impulsively seizing her hands folded now upon her Bible and fervently wishing— oh, how she wished it!—that Miss Tiddle's heart were weaker, or her gall bladder obstreperous, or her arteries hard, like her life. "But just at this minute, Annie, you're of more importance to me than the cards. Melvina Rust —bless her heart!—is inviting you to a tea party at three o'clock today, and it will take just *you* to make it a perfect occasion."

"At three?" asked Miss Tiddle, drawing her hands from Emma Davis' hold upon them and retreating farther into her chair. "Three o'clock will be impossible for me, I'm sorry to say. My time is short. I have a pressing engagement at just four."

"Time is always short for all of us, isn't it?" Emma Davis said, staring from the window at the little tree, which just then in a gentle whiff of wind tossed a few more petals on its shadow. "There's never time enough for all we want to do, and especially when we want to do things for others. I used to wonder, even when I was nine years old, at all the things you somehow

58

managed to do for us in your crowded days. You always seemed somehow to find time. I used to say to my mother, 'I don't see how Miss Tiddle does it.' This party will be very short itself, I'm sure, but very gay, too, for Mrs. Rust has just heard the most exciting thing about her nephew, Melvin, and a few of her very best friends are celebrating with her."

Miss Tiddle set her Bible suddenly down upon her table with what, in kindest words, must be recorded as a brisk and even angry slap. She eyed Miss Davis sharply.

"Melvina's been confused in her head for days," she said briefly. "Haven't we all noticed it? Don't we all know about that house of hers and about where that Melvin's been for all these years?"

"None of us ever knows everything about anything," Emma Davis said gently. "Every day I find I know next to nothing about most things. And if dear Rusty has been—shall we admit it, Annie, just between ourselves?—a bit confused, aren't we all confused some time or other? I assure you she's not confused about Melvin. He's come to himself at last. Rusty's received good tidings of great joy, Annie, just as it says in your Bible, which you know so well and have always lived by. And, knowing you as I do, I know you'll want to rejoice with her, even if you can spare only a brief quarter of an hour. She needs you, and you've never forsaken a friend in need; *that* I know from long experience. She said to me just now, 'I do hope Annie Tiddle can come. Then we'll be sure of a perfect party.' "

Miss Tiddle sat forward a bit in her chair. She was clearly both touched and embarrassed, and in her obvious confusion she fingered the cover of her Bible on the table, shuffling the first pages nervously.

"I haven't a thing to wear," she said at last. "My clothes are packed."

"Nonsense!" cried Emma Davis. "As though *you* wouldn't look nice in anything! That dress you have on right now is perfect for all occasions. I'll tell you what. I'll just bring around that new white collar of mine, you know the one, wide with all that lovely tatting which Mrs. Whipple made for me. That will add the finishing touch to this nice dress, and we'll maybe stick a flower on somewhere. Annie, dear, I knew you'd never fail me after years of helpfulness."

Miss Tiddle slowly and gravely took her Bible again into her lap.

"Melvina must realize, however," she said, "that my stay will be necessarily brief."

"Of course," Emma Davis said, rising from her chair and feeling for just an instant a bit unsteady even on her broad white feet. "Of course, Annie. But some people manage to *make* a party just by looking in on it. And that's *you!*"

11

MRS. SIGRID CHRISTIANSON'S ROOM WAS only three doors away from Annie Tiddle's, but in the few steps between them Emma Davis ousted from her mind everything but stark and ruthless necessity. "On, Emma, on!" she cried sternly to herself, for she was plainly *Emma* at this moment, with all openings firmly closed, not a vista discernible, not a garden gate ajar. She walked straight past Miss Sophonisba Clark's open door, not pausing to encourage Sophonisba, who, she well knew, was unsuccessfully striving to put the finishing touches on a paper entitled *Noble Women of the Old Testament* to be read at her literary club; past Mrs. Wilcox's, whose agitation

Emma could feel shaking itself into the corridor; past the large double room occupied by the Misses Wood, who were knitting silently and more rapidly than usual in their chairs before their two open windows.

When she reached Mrs. Christianson's door, she was not surprised to find it closed. It bore no sign of any kind. It was simply a closed door. Emma Davis knew as certainly as though she had turned the knob that it was locked as well. She was aware also that her startled knowledge was shared by Miss Sophonisba Clark, by Mrs. Wilcox, by the Wood sisters, silent in their rooms; and it was that ominous and common knowledge there in the still, sunswept corridor which left her motionless, and indeed suddenly mindless, in front of that locked door. Then, before she had time to search for her mind, she heard a key being slowly turned in the lock. The key made a high, querulous, ragged circle of sound, which, instead of terrifying Emma, had the odd result of bringing back her strayed senses to her, complete and unimpaired.

"Oil!" she said to herself in the brief moment before the door slowly opened. "All these pesky locks need oil." And the very image of the tiny spout of an oil can inserted in a lock, following the rectangular lines of a creaking bolt, of her thumb pressing the bottom of the can to release those yellow drops which should heal and calm that harsh scream of metal, brought healing and calm to Emma Davis herself.

Mrs. Sigrid Christianson swung wide her door, released her hold upon its knob, folded her large arms with their still powerful hands gripping her broad shoulders, and stared at Emma Davis out of large, pale blue eyes, which unmistakably held suspicion, resentment, and hostility.

"Always listening at folks' doors," she said in a high, hoarse whisper. "Always creeping about to find out folks' secrets. Don't I know? Can't I tell when someone's outside my door? I don't need to hear footsteps. I *know!*"

How big she is! Emma thought. What great, round eyes she has! The long forgotten, yet familiar words seemed to come from somewhere far back in her childhood, and although at the moment she couldn't trace their source, the understanding that they had been sitting comfortably inside her for many years somehow lent her a singular confidence and security. She laughed at Mrs. Christianson.

"If you couldn't hear *my* footsteps," she said

lightly, "you *must* be stone deaf. Size 9, width C, and no chance yet to get rubber heels on these new shoes. And as for listening, Christy, dear, I just haven't time for it this morning, much as I always love to hear you talk. I'm more full of news than the daily paper. I'm sure you won't mind my coming in for just five minutes. No more, I promise you." And before Mrs. Sigrid Christianson had time to unfold her arms in their black and white checked percale sleeves, Emma Davis had somehow wedged herself between the doorframe and Mrs. Christianson and had crossed the room to the window.

Mrs. Christianson did not follow her guest into her room. Instead she turned on her large feet in their black felt slippers like a slowly revolving mannequin and continued to stand in her open doorway and to stare at Emma Davis. I know now, Emma thought. I've got it. It was *Little Red Riding Hood* years back. That's what it was. *What great eyes you have, grandmother!*

She could not see the plum tree from the window, for Mrs. Christianson's room was on the back side of the Home for Aged Women. Instead she looked out on an expanse of lawn, which sloped downward toward another street

64

and which, unlike the front lawn, she noted, sadly needed its first spring mowing. Shall Angelina and I ever be able to afford a gasoline mower? thought Emma. And the very dream of that mower in some distant future, its quick, compact *putt-putts* as it swept across the grass, as it left wide swaths of firm, shorn turf, somehow gave her an absurd courage to turn from the window and to meet Mrs. Christianson's pale blue gaze again, which in the meantime she had felt unmistakably between her shoulder blades.

There was a large table just to the left of Mrs. Christianson's window, and on it Emma Davis saw, in the fleeting moments when her eyes somehow failed to meet Mrs. Christianson's eyes, an amazing array of scissors in varying sizes, all neatly placed in a shining row, their handles, circular, oval, cylindrical, plumb with the table edge, their blades, long and thin like lancets, heavy and thick, round-edged and dull, extending in uneven ranks toward the center of the table. Wherever, asked Emma Davis' mind, now fortunately with her, did she get all those scissors? But she was almost instantly diverted from that subject of research by the quick and alarming discovery that she did not need to continue it. Instead she looked beyond the scissors to dozens of scattered pictures, photographs, magazine illustrations, which Mrs. Christianson had been evidently mounting on large sheets of brown paper. The pictures were all of snow: snow scenes in New England woods, falling snow, snow-covered lonely hills beyond empty plains—in Iceland, in the Dakotas, in Sweden?—snow-capped, jagged mountain peaks. Were they the Rockies, the Alps, the Himalayas? Or were they in the Antarctic, a favorite subject of the *National Geographic*—that land of night and of unbelievable, relentless cold?

As Emma Davis hastily scanned the snow on Mrs. Christianson's table, Mrs. Christianson herself advanced a step farther into her room, and with her advance Emma again met her eyes. They are like cold and snow themselves, she thought, bleak, bitter, frightening.

"I see you like snow," she said, a bit feebly, it must be admitted.

"I hate it!" Mrs. Christianson said.

Emma gathered herself swiftly together.

"All these lovely pictures then must be for presents for your friends, for people who do like snow."

"They're not," said Mrs. Christianson.

"They're to paper my room, to make me feel like my old home."

"What a nice idea!" cried Emma Davis. "And when you've put them all up, for these walls do need re-doing, as I told Miss Norton only yesterday, you'll give a party, just like Mrs. Rust this afternoon, and let us all see your new room.

"I shan't do any such thing!" said Mrs. Christianson.

Emma Davis stood by the table with her back to the window and looked steadily at the old woman, who had now moved nearer the center of the room. She was seeking for some faint gleam of friendliness, of confidence, in Mrs. Christianson's eyes, but she found none; she was searching in her own mind for something to say, something which might banish even for an instant the enveloping darkness and defeat in that small room. She found nothing but a pity that could not be uttered or even made evident.

It's all been a mistake, she thought. Angelina was right two years ago. It was too late then, only where could she have gone? Where do old people go when there's no one left to care for them? Just where?

It was quite too late, thought Emma Davis

again, after all those many years out on those plains, in the shadow of those mountains— Montana, was it? Wyoming? Homesteading— was that what they called it fifty years ago?— taking up land, those vast, neighborless stretches of country, obscured by blizzards, burned by August heat, ravaged by cyclones and thunderstorms. Those eager, anxious groups of strangers, Bohemians, Austrians, Swedes, far from their close, friendly towns, their gay cities, Prague, Vienna, Stockholm, separated now from one another by miles of land, carrying about with them the memories of home, traditions, and customs, old, long ways of life, learning new manners, becoming gladly alienated or forever sad.

"She couldn't take it," Mrs. Christianson's only son had said of her, when, defeated himself after years of discouragement, he had brought her back with a girl, a schoolteacher, who had madly gone out there to teach and more madly married Nils Christianson. "But she'll be all right here with you. All she needs is to have a few womenfolks around." The schoolteacher had supplied the money for the Home, and then she and Nils had gone, far beyond any reach of Angelina's frantic inquiries.

Emma Davis understood at that moment that, like Mrs. Christianson, she had had more than she could take. I'm licked, she thought. I'm plain beaten. The problem now is how I'm going to get out of here with her dreadful eyes on me.

Mrs. Christianson moved forward then until she was quite close to Emma Davis. She unfolded her large arms, dropped them from her shoulders, and suddenly clasped her big, mottled hands together. She needs a bath, thought Emma, and that black and white percale, it's filthy. Perhaps it was the very untidiness of Mrs. Christianson or the vision of her soaking in a tub, homely pictures like those of the oil can and the new lawn mower, which freed Emma's tongue; perhaps it was the sudden dropping of Mrs. Christianson's arms, the pathos of her clasped hands; or perhaps she saw, or at least imagined that she saw, the merest flicker of interest, or even of need, in Mrs. Christianson's pale eyes. At all events, her tongue was loosened, and she began to speak, if not in inspired utterances, at least in natural ones.

"I didn't mean to stay, my dear," she said, "and I'm awfully sorry to keep you from such interesting work. I just popped in for Melvina

Rust to invite you to a tea party at just three o'clock this afternoon in her room. You'll learn the why of it at dinner in just about an hour from now. I do hope you can manage to come at just three. You'll add so much to Melvina's happiness."

Mrs. Christianson dismissed the pleasantry.

"I shan't eat my dinner today," she said briefly. "And I thought tea parties were at four o'clock. I'm busy today at four, and at three I'll be deciding what to do when the clock strikes four."

"We all seem busy today at four," Emma Davis said brightly. "That's why Mrs. Rust decided on three; but come if you possibly can, won't you?" Before she started for the door, she put both her hands impulsively on the clenched ones of Mrs. Christianson and smiled into her pale, distraught eyes. "We'll all miss you if you decide you can't spare the time."

Mrs. Christianson stood, tall and massive in her ugly dress, looking down upon Emma Davis like some disheveled Norse Fury, biding her time.

"I think I can spare it," she said, carefully shaping each laden word. "I might even decide what to do right there at that party."

12

The DINNER ON THE 15TH OF MAY IN the Home for Aged Women was a complete success, a gala occasion, indeed, if there ever was one. Everyone dressed up for it (except Miss Norton and Miss Davis, with whom no one would feel really at home except in navy blue and white), and the black dresses were enlivened by a white fichu here and a white frill there; everyone for that brief hour valiantly laid aside, or stifled, any feelings of nervous tension and strain, which accomplishment was made more possible by Mrs. Christianson's unmentioned absence. Mrs. Rust, perilously near to tears from pride and happiness, sat proudly at Emma Davis' right, and Miss Tiddle, with Mrs. Whipple's cascade of tatting enlivening her rather somber dress, at Angelina Norton's. There were sprays of plum blossoms on the three tables, which were so put together that everyone felt like a family, and place cards, and even crepe-paper hats in various colors, which all put on with great glee, although Miss Tiddle had to be urged a bit before she did so. The three roast chickens came in whole instead of being mangled in the kitchen as they usually were; and someone had tied jaunty pink bows on the six upright legs, which absurdity made everyone laugh and laugh.

While Miss Norton carved them (and, indeed, throughout the entire meal), Miss Davis told story after story, each funnier than the last. She told about how, when she was a little girl, she had given her cow snuff, and how the cow had nearly sneezed to death; and how once on Commonwealth Avenue, Boston, when she was sixteen and was paying her first and only visit to that city, she had stepped over a huge dog lying on the pavement, and how the dog had gotten up just at the wrong instant and moved off with Miss Davis right on his back, to the immense embarrassment of Miss Davis and to the vast amusement of much of Boston. She told about a girl she had known in her childhood who, in return for a penny or a stick of striped candy, would recklessly swallow any required number of pins and who had never known the least discomfort from them; and about a boy named Austin Kneebone—yes, that was truly his name—whose joints were so supple and so flexible that he could snap his bones in and out, down and up, at his friends' eager requests, giving himself meanwhile such grotesque contours and strange protuberances that he looked for all the world like a relief map.

They all said they hadn't laughed so much in years, and old Mrs. Whipple said she'd had enough to laugh over all the rest of her life. Even Miss Sophonisba Clark unbent enough to ask three puzzling riddles; and Mrs. Wilcox contributed the funniest of limericks to the surprise and delight of all. The ice-cream roses charmed everyone, as did the green shamrocks, and Mrs. O'Neill, who brought little Agnes' shining medal to the table, managed to enjoy hers without a single *Glory be to God*.

Just at the close Miss Norton rose and made a little speech. She sent a confidential glance, as she began, around among the Seventies, who smiled back at her in complete understanding. She said that, since they all might wonder why this gala dinner, she would tell them briefly of all the things which had put it into her mind. First of all, she said, it was the spring itself which, as everyone knew, always suggested gaiety and laughter, and especially that little plum tree out there on the lawn which she hoped they had all seen. That little tree, she said, had just cried out for a party. Then there was Mrs. Rust's wonderful gift, which they had all seen on the table by the door, from her nephew Melvin way from Tokyo, Japan, where he was undoubtedly making a name for himself to his aunt's glory and honor. Lastly, there were certain plans of certain members of the family which might just possibly mean absence for a season; and she thought she would just seize the time when everybody was together to have a really memorable party. Then, just before Mrs. Rust and Miss Tiddle had a chance to say what Angelina Norton and Emma Davis saw on their faces getting ready to be said, she proposed that they all sing "Auld Lang Syne," because there was no better way to end a lovely occasion than by an old, familiar song which everybody knew. Emma Davis clapped her hands loudly then, and they all, except Mrs. Whipple, rose and sang, with Emma leading in a safe, low pitch, and then she clapped her hands again and cried, "Rest time for us all!" which made them scurry into the hall with their paper caps still on and make for their rooms.

13

AT A QUARTER PAST ONE, WHEN THE Home for Aged Women at least seemed quiet, except for the thought of what might be seething behind Mrs. Christianson's locked door, when Angelina had been persuaded to lie down for an hour, and when that early afternoon somnolence had descended upon the street, the lawn, and the plum tree, Emma Davis wheeled her bicycle from behind the green latticework underneath the high front porch and prepared to mount it for her journey up the hill to see Susan Pierce at the State Hospital. She still wore her white uniform and cap, for she had not had a moment in this mad, this outlandish, this dreadful day to divest herself of anything save utter panic or to put on anything save her old blue nurse's cape and a fragment of hope that the tardy arrival of four o'clock might not witness widespread ruin, irreparable not only to Melvina Rust, Annie Tiddle, and Sigrid Christianson, but to the present and the future of the Home for Aged Women.

When she raised her right leg to mount her bicycle, to press the pedal with the broad sole of her white oxford, she wished fervently that she were lying face downward on her bed and that someone, preferably herself, were giving her a good back rub. Why she was lame she could not conceive, but lame she surely was. The calves of her legs sang with complaint, as though tight wires vibrated within them; the

75

sciatic nerve in her right thigh twinged with pain; the space between her shoulder blades throbbed and ached, sending pulsating quivers along the taut cords of her neck; even her fingers on her handle bars were stiff and awkward. Yes, a good rub would work wonders; not Angelina's rub, for Angelina was too well bred, too delicate, too tentative, worked too much and too lightly with her fingers and not enough with the flat of her hands. Her own rub was what she wanted. How often had she glowed with pardonable pride over the groans of ecstatic pleasure which her back rubs had drawn throughout the years! First, the strong, firm movements of the palms, even of the heels of her broad, capable hands, forth and back, up and down, from the coccyx to the nape of the neck; then the wide, steady, circular motions, extending far to the sides, raising, revolving the flesh in resolute thumb and fingers, seizing it, pinching and kneading it as one kneads bread; the rotating grasp with strong fingertips upon those taut cords of the neck; the deft manipulation of every tired, tense vertebra, every cramped muscle, every hidden nerve. How well she knew each strong and skillful motion! How welcome at that moment would be her own hands upon her own aching self!

Well, since that was not to be, she would get along on her way with just a glance at the plum tree, for time was precious. There it stood, its darkened shadow under the midday sun hugging it closely, the dew now dried upon its frail, wide-open blossoms, a white petal, as she looked, drifting idly down through the bright, luminous air. Was it but a tree, she wondered, remembering the madness it had engendered, the buying of the tea set so like itself, the quick framing of lies; recalling the way it had become Hawley, the awe with which the little girls had gazed upon it. Somewhere, she dimly thought, she had heard that spirits dwelt in trees, once mortals on this earth, then trunks and branches, leaves and blossoms, yet still able to exert strange power. Perhaps, indeed, some mysterious force or essence hidden in that white mist of bloom was prompting her, when, like Angelina, she might be lying flat on her bed, to pedal her bicycle as far as she could pedal it up the long hill toward those grim buildings on its crest.

Her front wheel became jittery far sooner than usual as she pedaled up the hill. The calves of her legs early cried out to her to free them. She felt herself more than a little out of breath as, dismounting, she pushed her bicycle up the steep incline toward the stone gates and on between them along the walk which led to the main women's building. Susan Pierce would be there, waiting for her in her office to the right of the great entrance door, smoking too many cigarettes, looking at Emma Davis with stern, yet kind gray eyes, not thinking Emma quite a fool, quite a blithering idiot, as she herself often feared she was.

"What have you done now, Davy?" Susan would say. "Out with it! I'm sure it's quite wrong and entirely right."

Susan Pierce was there. She had been there in the same chair for many years, seeing endless anxious people, studying strange eyes, watching for countless forbidding signs. She gave Emma Davis a cigarette. They smoked together for a few quiet minutes. She had rooms ready for Melvina Rust and Annie Tiddle, she told Emma then, next to each other, looking out upon fields and trees. She feared that Mrs. Christianson must go elsewhere for a time, but who knew what might be done even for Mrs. Christianson? She did not at all object to a tea set, although such paraphernalia was usually not admitted with its owners, although she might think best to keep it in her own room for just a bit. She would herself have a cup of tea now and then with Mrs. Rust, talk with her about 14 Vine Street; and she would not forget on holidays to send Miss Tiddle a flowered card with an appreciative sentiment. Yes, Emma Davis might come to see them as often as she liked, but only providing—and, remember, Davy, I'm a woman of my word!—only providing that she sleep tonight ten hours on end, after a stiff drink, which she, Susan Pierce, had, knowing Angelina, already hidden for Emma in a deceptive cretonne knitting bag.

14

EMMA DAVIS FELT IMMEASURABLY BETter once she had talked with Susan Pierce and smoked three of her cigarettes. There was just one thing that she still needed, if she could only spare the time—just one thing which would take the ache from her legs, loosen the tightness from her neck and shoulders, straighten out her still confused mind, prepare her for anyone's four o'clock. She glanced at her Ingersoll on her left wrist as she mounted her bicycle outside Susan's office. It said ten minutes past two. Only one half-hour, she thought, only thirty minutes but —*Enough.*

When she had swooped down the steep incline between the State Hospital gates, she did not swing rashly to the left and coast down the long hill. Instead she bumped straight ahead for a hundred yards along a rough lane until the front wheel of her bicycle was halted by some bars which gave entrance to a high pasture. She knew the pasture well, for she had gone berrying there as a small child before there was any State Hospital or, for that matter, any Home for Aged Women. She knew that, once she had left her bicycle at the bars and woven her way for the length of another hundred yards among the gray rocks, the new ferns, and the purple of opening lambkill, she would reach a ledge covered with lichen and sheltered by rough spruces. There, quite by herself, clothed and wrapped in her generous years, their dark nights, their opening days, their tragedies and their brief triumphs (which is the only clothing we have, indeed, the only identity), she could give herself the one indulgence which she craved—the necessary, unfettered, absurd, and refreshing cry of her life.

How long was it, she asked herself, as she stumbled among the rocks on her way to the ledge, since she had really cried? Since she had

80

either been able to afford the time or to find the right place? She really could not remember how long it had been. A Home for Aged Women provided the poorest environment for such a luxury. Moreover, to Angelina tears were tears, puzzling and upsetting; they were neither freeing streams nor healing springs.

Once she reached the ledge, she spread her cape on the gray lichen so that her white uniform might not bear telltale evidences of her utter abandonment, took off her shoes so that her swollen feet might have their reward also, stretched herself at full length, face downward, and began to cry. In less than a minute she was in the blessed thick of it. Her aching shoulders shook with sobs; the tight muscles of her neck and throat gave way before them; her diaphragm heaved upward and with every lurch within her let loose streams of tears. Her eyelids reddened and swelled; her mouth quivered and trembled; her nose ran; the lines and furrows of her face filled with tiny rills of water which spilled out upon the red lining of her cape and lay there in soaked dark splotches; her large handkerchief was powerless against the deluge and soon became a sopping rag.

She cried, first, for the pain of that one day, those few laden hours. For Annie Tiddle's

81

starved life, which she had hoped to feed and nourish and could not; for Rusty's red geranium, her polyanthus, her apple dowdy; for Sigrid Christianson's fear on those vast plains under the awful shadow of those towering mountains. For Angelina's patience with her lies, her silly hopes and dreams, her mad extravagance. She cried for Miss Tiddle's strong heart, her young arteries; for the queer sadness of those pink bows on the legs of those chickens; for old Mrs. Whipple in a crepe-paper sunbonnet. For the little girls, hand in hand, gazing at the plum tree, for the new light and life which they must sometime, somehow, endure.

Then she cried over the past, for all the years she had known, no longer in the far distance, but now pulsating within her. Over Hawley, her vision, her kindness, her laughter, her death somewhere in France, in a base hospital at Verdun, or Château Thierry, or the Argonne. Over loneliness and bewilderment and defeat; over young death and too persistent life; over faltering tongues and unspoken words. A rush of tears welled up over the memory of an awkward country boy who longed to hold his mother's hand and could not. Another deluge over an old colored man who said one word over and over again for a full week before he died, until they all went half crazy. "Yes, yes," that old man said. "Yes, yes." What did he mean by that affirmation? Or did he mean nothing at all? What did anything mean? asked Emma Davis, sobbing face downward on her ledge in the warm afternoon sunlight.

And as though she had not cried enough, as though the blows and the bruises, the wounds and the wrongs which she had seen and known in forty years were not enough to draw forth her tears, she found herself sobbing over the lovely things that she had known. Do tears alone hold life together in one encompassing bond, from birth to death, from generation to generation? Her tears fell over her life with Angelina; all its problems shared together; all its wild dreams of Spain and Stratford-on-Avon, perhaps more satisfying because unrealized in their outward forms; all its fun. They fell over the old, their little courtesies, their frequent wisdom, their gratitude, their long patience. They fell over walks in the country on rare, untroubled afternoons, over sunrises and sunsets, quiet nights of rain. Over unwise or startling presents, an electric blanket for Angelina's neuritis, a bright red sweater for Emma—how she had loved it!—a lipstick for Angelina—Davy, I *can't* use it! I wouldn't *dare*—a plated silver service, bought on payments for the evening cocoa parties. Over the pair of thrushes which had come to their back lawn the first week in May for thirty years, giving them painful delight at each arrival, nesting there, rearing their awkward, speckled young. Over the plum tree—a rush of tears over the plum tree—which every spring lent wings to their feet and strength to their hands, symbolizing for them eternal youth, desire, and hope.

But even as she cried, Emma Davis had an eye on her watch, on her trusty old Ingersoll, which, guaranteed for one year only, had gone on generously for five. When the hands of that watch said two thirty-five, she sat up, put on her shoes, shook the moss and lichen from her damp cape, and refastened her distorted cap to her thinning hair. Five minutes remained, and not a second more, for her to summon up courage for Mrs. Rust's tea party and for that tragic hour of four o'clock which could no longer be averted.

Then an odd thing happened to her, sitting on that ledge, surrounded by that warm sunlight. She suddenly found that she did not need to summon up courage; she all at once discovered that courage was here, stout and strong within her. All she needed to do was to sit there during the blessed loan of those five minutes, in the sunlight, grateful for her cry, grateful for her forty years, every one of them spent —could one deny it?—with trouble and sorrow, illness, old age, and death.

She did not define the gifts of those years, the visions she had seen, the truths which had been borne in upon her; perhaps she did not even think about them at all, for Emma Davis was not one given to analysis, speculation, or reflection; but she knew them. They lay within her, undefined, yet understood, intangible, yet real. The gift of illness, which, through the years, she had slowly realized, the awakened sense of its revealing power, of its unexploited mine of wealth. Long days of catching up with life, holding it in one's quiet hands, looking at it with surprise, aware at last, if one ever is aware, of its meaning. The gift of gay pretense, a game to be played day by day, hour by hour, with oneself, with one's anxious friends, with fear of the future, with foolish panic at the thought of death, that quiet, common lot, that way of all the earth—until one day the game was won, and pretense had quite simply become transcended into truth. The freedom which acceptance brings; the new understanding of time, no longer as a possession to be tightly held and jealously guarded, but rather as a loan from the beginning, to be invested in life itself; in the falling of a yellow leaf, the afternoon light on a stone wall; in the words of the day and the wisdom of the night; in the unassailable knowledge of those who, waiting upon God, can run and not be weary, can walk and not faint.

Two-forty, warned the trusty Ingersoll. Emma bounded from the ledge, hurried over the rocks and through the new ferns, turned her bicycle from the pasture bars, wheeled it to the summit of the long hill. She mounted it; then, in a mad, unconquerable impulse, after half a dozen quick revolutions of her wheels, she swept down the hill. She relinquished her hold upon her handle bars and threw her arms far out to right and left. Her old blue cape with its red lining streamed behind her like a banner. Down she went, gathering speed at every moment, exultant, reckless, safe. Shall I, or shan't I? she thought, as she neared the Home for Aged Women at the foot of the hill. I shall! And without touching her handle bars, without slackening her speed, she swung her body at exactly the right, the discreet, the prudent angle and sailed up the asphalt walk of the Home toward Angelina Norton, who was transfixed on the topmost step of the porch.

"What in the world have you been up to?" cried Angelina, when Emma had abruptly halted her flight by suddenly dropping her extended foot on the lowest step. "Haven't you a grain of sense left? You're a fright! You look as if you had a good case of poison ivy!"

"No," Emma Davis said, as she hauled away her bicycle toward the door in the lattice. "No, Angelina. I haven't. I've had a wonderful time, and I never felt better in all my life!"

15

AT EXACTLY FIVE MINUTES TO THREE o'clock Angelina Norton and Emma Davis climbed the stairs to go to old Mrs. Rust's tea party.

"Hold on tight, Angelina!" Emma Davis said. "There's only one more hour to weather."

"But it's the fatal one," Angelina said. "Anything may happen before four o'clock. They promised they'd come early, just in case. I do

think you've overdone things a bit, Davy—
that tea set, that Melvin hoax, this crazy party.
The dinner would have been enough; but
you've always been a bit silly over Rusty."

"Perhaps," Emma Davis said. "But old
Rusty's been my pal for years, and take it from
me she won't be on Vine Street or anywhere
else too much longer. Rusty hasn't had too
many breaks in her life either. Now you just
follow my lead, Angelina, and tonight you're
getting a pill with a long sleep at the end of it.
As for me," she concluded firmly and without
the least embarrassment, "I'm seriously thinking of getting somewhat drunk."

"That's quite all right by me," said Angelina, so calmly that Emma Davis was taken by
surprise. "You can't for a minute think that
I'm such a fool as not to know what's in that
knitting bag."

Emma Davis seized Angelina's hand then
in a rare gesture of affection. She thought at
that moment that if Life would only let her
and Angelina go on together for a few more
years, five more in the Home until they got
things where they wanted them, five more, say,
in their apartment until Shakespeare was mas-
tered, until they had had time for all those

88

bountiful things they wanted to do, until they had had a dog of their own to tousle and walk and be silly over—if Life would just do this for her and Angelina, she would, in truth, want for nothing.

16

OLD MRS. RUST WAS READY FOR HER party. She was dressed in lavender with a strong odor of toilet water about her. She sat on the edge of her chair with her new tea set on the table before her. She had put on her black hat, and her black coat and gloves were folded neatly on the bulging carryall at the foot of her bed. Her room looked rather bare, but her early guests made no comment. The teakettle on the electric plate was beginning to hum.

"How nice you do look, Mrs. Rust!" Miss Norton said. "That lavender is just the color for you."

"Thank you kindly," Mrs. Rust said. "Nobody can look too nice when she's going back home after many years."

"That's true, Rusty," Miss Davis said.

"That's very true. And here, right on the dot, are Mrs. Christianson and Miss Tiddle."

Mrs. Christianson had clearly made no personal preparations for Mrs. Rust's party. She was still wearing her black and white checked percale, and she was still, Emma Davis thought, in need of a bath. Nevertheless, Emma's anxious scrutiny revealed nothing about her more alarming than general frowsiness and ill nature, and she felt a vast wave of relief. When Mrs. Christianson was once in the room, she greeted no one at all. Instead she went straight to the best chair by the window, sat down in it, folded her hands, and gazed into space. Then she said to nobody in particular and in anything but a party tone:

"What's this yollification for?"

Annie Tiddle answered her question. Miss Tiddle had parted her white hair neatly on one side and encircled it in a youthful fashion with a band of black velvet ribbon. She was still wearing Mrs. Whipple's tatting around the neck of her black dress; and, since she had put some rouge rather badly on her cheeks and wore a pink rosebud pinned to her shoulder, she looked definitely partyish, although there was a strained, tired look about her brown eyes and a constant nervous twitch in her eyebrows which made everyone who saw her feel a bit insecure. Also, since she carried a watch clutched in her left hand and peeked at it at least every ten seconds, she did not add to that delightful sense of ease and leisure which all tea parties should emanate. But, unlike Mrs. Christianson, she was doing her best to make Mrs. Rust's party a success, and she was politeness itself as from her perch on the foot of Mrs. Rust's bed she answered Mrs. Christianson.

"It's for good cheer, I'm sure," she said, "and I think it's very kind of Mrs. Rust to invite us."

"Not at all, Annie dear," Mrs. Rust answered. "It's easy to be kind to one's old friends."

Mrs. Christianson moved a little in her chair and cleared her throat ominously. Then she said slowly to the sunny world outside the open window:

"Kindness would die a natural death if justice were once established on this earth."

This unexpected pronouncement, which seemed to have no conceivable relationship to Mrs. Christianson as her friends had known her for the past two years, came as something of a shock to all; but Emma Davis rallied magnificently.

"What a wonderful thought, Mrs. Christianson!" she cried. "And how very wise! Now let me write that down for my quotation book. It's lucky I always have my pen and pad right with me. Do repeat it, please."

"No," said Mrs. Christianson. "I won't."

"Never mind," Emma Davis said. "I've got it down, and I shall always remember it. It's something everyone ought to think about. Yes, Rusty, the tea is ready, I'm sure. Miss Tiddle, how will you take your tea?"

"Just as it comes, please," Miss Tiddle said politely, looking at her watch. "And if you collect quotations, Miss Davis, I've one for you that I found in an anthology of the world's best literature. *In the midst of life we are in death.*

"Thank you, Annie, dear," Miss Davis said, reopening her pen. "That's new to me, and very true, too. Now here's your tea. Aren't Mrs. Rust's cups lovely? And Miss Norton has a cookie there right by your elbow."

"How will you have your tea, Mrs. Christianson?" asked old Mrs. Rust. She had the feeling that things were not going as they ought with Mrs. Christianson, and she asked the question very warmly and graciously.

"I won't," said Mrs. Christianson. "I never drink tea. It don't agree with me."

"That's just what I thought at the last moment, Mrs. Christianson," Emma Davis said. "I know Swedish people set great store by coffee, and I brought along some of the instant kind, powder, of course, but very good, too. Now, Rusty, one of your cups and that nice boiling water, and we'll fix Mrs. Christianson up in a jiffy. If you don't like tea, you just don't. I never could drink milk in spite of all the doctors say, and I, a nurse, too; but there you are. I can't bear the taste of milk."

Emma Davis experienced more than a mere qualm as she handed Mrs. Christianson the coffee, and she was immensely relieved when Mrs. Christianson began a bit noisily to drink it.

"I do hope it's good," she said with real concern.

"It's only fair," said Mrs. Christianson.

"You've hardly touched your own tea, Rusty," Emma Davis said, "and it's your party. Angelina, don't keep all those cookies to yourself. And, Miss Tiddle, couldn't you manage better if you put your watch on the bed? You can see it from there, I'm sure."

"Thank you," Miss Tiddle said. "I prefer to keep it by me. I must watch the time."

"Now that we're all settled comfortably,"

93

Emma Davis said, "and having *such* a good time, Rusty, I'm wondering if Mrs. Christianson wouldn't tell us something about Sweden. It's a country we all know too little about, and so important to us all since the war. Don't you remember, Mrs. Christianson, at those games we played last winter—you remember, lotto, tiddledywinks, and parchesi—how you told us about that bear you killed, when you were only sixteen, with your father's gun when he came prowling around your sheep pens. It was such an exciting story that I'm sure we'd all love to hear it again."

Angelina sent Emma a warning glance then, but it was sent just too late. Emma tried frantically to retrieve her stupid, fatal error, to think of something, *anything*, which would steer Mrs. Christianson's addled, frenzied wits toward the safe and the relatively sane. She found nothing, absolutely nothing in her mind but defeat and terror. She turned in desperation toward Angelina, to find no means of rescue in her startled face. She saw Mrs. Christianson sit up straight in her chair; she watched her set her coffee cup slowly down upon the floor; she helplessly waited there in that tense silence while Mrs. Christianson rose

94

to her feet and turned her large, pale eyes upon them all.

"It was not a bear that I killed," she said. She spoke quietly, her words conveying a promise of many more to follow, just as before a summer storm the air is laden, ominous, and still. "It was a man. I killed him with a bread knife from my mother's kitchen. I've—"

Suddenly, at the last possible moment, there leaped into Emma Davis' empty mind one of those unpredictable, inconsequential images which have saved so many of us when all has seemed quite lost. Like the oil can and the lawn mower, like Red Riding Hood, like Mrs. Christianson in the tub, it flew into her head with rescue and healing on its prosaic wings. It was nothing else than tiddledywinks, those absurd little disks in a row, red, blue, yellow, green, white, on that piece of felt, snapped by fumbling old hands, toward that silly pot in the middle of the table, falling off the edge, rolling into obscure corners of the room. At the very sight of those tiddledywinks there in her mind, Emma laughed outright, a burst of laughter which, resounding in the surcharged room, drew forth hysterical echoes from Angelina, bewildered titters from Melvina Rust, and even a nervous refrain from Annie Tiddle.

Everyone, in fact, contributed her frightened bit to this unexpected merriment except Mrs. Christianson.

"Those tiddledywinks!" Emma Davis cried. "Those silly tiddledywinks! Do you remember that night, Rusty, when you snapped a tiddledywink straight into Annie's cocoa? Wasn't it funny, Annie, dear? Shall we ever forget it? You remember that night, don't you, Mrs. Christianson?"

"No," said Mrs. Christianson. "I don't. And you interrupted me. I was just telling you about how, at four o'clock—"

Then instantly, if not with forethought, yet just in time to halt any further confidences from Mrs. Christianson, Annie Tiddle did her part to retrieve the day and to conserve old Mrs. Rust's tea party from disaster.

"Speaking of four o'clock," she said quickly, "it's getting on toward four now, and I really must go. I'm sure it's been a beautiful party, Mrs. Rust, and let me congratulate you on your nephew Melvin. Now a long good-by, and God bless us all, for the hour cometh and now is." And Miss Tiddle started for the door.

"Just one minute, Annie, dear!" Emma Davis called. "Just one little minute! Before we leave this nice party, let's all look at the plum tree, for it's full of the afternoon sun, and it's too lovely to miss. Let's all stand together by the window here, for it may rain tomorrow, and all the blossoms will fall."

Miss Tiddle obligingly returned from the door; Mrs. Christianson turned sullenly toward the window; Emma Davis guided old Mrs. Rust there; and Angelina stood behind them all, thinking of anything in the world except the little plum tree.

"Isn't it lovely?" Emma Davis cried. "Isn't it young and gay? And aren't we all lucky to have it right here on our very own lawn?"

Just at that moment, to Angelina Norton's unspeakable relief, while they all stood in Mrs. Rust's window space looking at the plum tree, a long black car drew up at the curb. It was a car which might suggest several purposes to imaginations open to suggestions, and that is precisely what it did do.

"It's for me!" Mrs. Rust cried. "I'm sorry, everybody, but I must be off!"

"I'm quite sure it's for me," Miss Tiddle cried, looking at her watch and twitching more than ever. "Only they've come earlier than I said. I don't quite know how I'm going to manage."

"You're all wrong," Mrs. Christianson said.

"I've been expecting it for days. They're after me at last."

Emma Davis and Angelina Norton managed to encircle all three of the old women with their strong arms, and by a mighty effort they managed also to keep from bursting into tears.

"The only way to discover whose car it is," Emma Davis said gaily, "is for us all to go down together and find out. And whosever car it is, Angelina and I are going right along. For it's a lovely afternoon for a drive, and no one can ever tell a thing about tomorrow."